# Teddy Bears
# Traveling Adventures

Designed By Roni Akmon
Compiled & Edited
By Nancy Akmon

Blushing Rose Publishing
San Anselmo, California

# About These Bears

When in the autumn of 1905, I created the characters of Teddy-B and Teddy-G, I built better than I knew. I brought these bears out of their mountain den in Colorado and started them on their tour of the East to teach children that animals, even bears, may have some measure of human feeling; that the primary purpose of animals is not necessarily that of supplying sport for the hunter. That this lesson has been abundantly taught is proven by the overwhelming welcome given the Teddy Bears by the boys and girls of the United States; and it is safe to say that the traditional "bear will get you" has now and forever lost its frightening significance.

--Seymour Eaton 1905

Designed by Roni Akmon
Compiled and edited by Nancy Akmon

Text by Seymour Eaton, with editing and new text by Nancy Akmon. Cover Illustration and interior illustrations by C.K.Culver and V. Floyd Cambell.
Certain line illustrations have been adapted for this book by Wendy Cogan.

Efforts have been made to find the copyright holders of material used in this publication.
We apologize for any omissions or errors and will be pleased to include the appropriate acknowledgements in future editions.

ISBN# 1-884807-50-X

Blushing Rose Publishing
P.O. Box 2238
San Anselmo, Ca. 94979
www.blushingrose.com
printed in China

# The Teddy Bears Leave Their Mountain Home

Two Teddy Bears had
a home out West,
in a big ravine near a
mountain crest,
where they ate their
meals and took
their rest,
and gathered
sunshine and strength
and cheer,
and welcomed friends
from far and near.

One Bear was black
and one was gray;
each was good and
neither would say
a swear word loud
either night or day.
In love and learning
they were both alike,
they could run a
motor or hike a bike.

These things they had
learned from papers lost
by weary travelers as
the hills they crossed.

They did things fair
and neither would bite
if neighbors tried to
do things right.

*"Two Teddy Bears had a home out West
In a big ravine near a mountain crest"*

The black bear's name was Teddy-B;
the B for black or brown you see,
or bright or bold or brave or boss:
he was always kind and seldom cross.
The gray bear's name was Teddy-G;
the G for grizzly or gray for he
was as full of fun as a bear can be.
Not B for bad and G for good
the black bear wanted it understood.

The "Teddy" part is a name they found
on hat and tree and leggings round,
on belt and boot, and plates of tin,
and scraps of paper and biscuits thin,
and other things that hunters drop
when they chase a bear to a mountain top.

*"They found some gold in a cave one day"*

"With bags on backs and sticks in hand,
They started their adventure across the land"

Their home was high and deep and wide, an elegant place for bears to hide the things picked up on the mountainside. They were well supplied with hats and boots, and leather coats and cowboy suits, and pots and pans and whips and strings, and belts and horns and a hundred things lost on the trail by hunters bold when driven home by the winter's cold.

These Bears some travel books had found, which told them that the world was round. They made up their minds that they would see & learn about geography. And visit cities everywhere and introduce the Teddy Bear.

They found some gold in a cave one day, which they could use to pay their way.

The Bears were tired of the life they led;
they wanted to see the world they said;
to visit New York and Boston too,
and perhaps Chicago and Kalamazoo;
to go to theatre and church and school,
to see a banker or broker, and swim in a pool.
With money a little and try a hand
at running a paper or leading a band.

They had heard of things bear's never see:
golf and weddings and afternoon tea,
trolleys and trains and buildings high,
and machines that write and machines that fly,
and the President and his eldest son,
and the Capitol at Washington;
and other things both great and small
that bears have never seen at all.

*"On a train out West, and playing a banjo song"*

"I won't sleep upstairs, said Teddy-G,
I want a window so I can see."

The story tells how
these Teddy Bears
scattered forever all
blues and cares,
and made fun and frolic
and mischief too,
and did some tricks
for bears quite new;

And how some folks,
the stories tell,
liked these two
Teddy Bears so well
that they made a
million for the
stores to sell.

Some quite little,
for children small,
and some as big
as the bears are tall.
The brown ones
looking like Teddy-B,
and the white ones as
funny as Teddy-G.

The story goes on to
tell how far these two
bears rode in a
Pullman car on the
train, and the tricks
they played on the
folks that night,
when the porter turned
out the light.

The news had scattered far and wide that the Bears would leave the mountain side, give away their goods and rent their trees, and travel East and beyond the seas. Their friends had gathered to feast and laugh and sigh, to give advice and say good-bye.

The lunch was through and the play was on, when a shot was heard from a hunter's gun. The guests were ordered to run and hide while the bears stepped out on the mountain side.

Teddy-B said to the hunter, who stood by the tree, " Hands up, you come with us; don't touch your gun or make a fuss."

The hunter was scared from head to toe, he dropped his gun and had to go.

After the hunters were introduced around
to all the guests upon the ground,
they were made to sign in red and white,
a bond the Bears prepared that night.
On birch-bark paper and sealed in gold, which read
like this in writing bold:
"We hereby take oath on bended knee, that from this
hour on we do agree, to keep the peace and hunting stop
from canyon deep to mountain top.
In weather fair, in snow or rain,
we'll never enter the Bears domain
or throw a stone or shoot again
at goat or game at bird or beast,
till the Bears returned from their journey East."

At break of day the hunters went: they left a
note which read they say:
"Dear bears we are off, good day.
We like you're home but we wouldn't stay,
for game or gold for pie or pay;
we are off for good; we won't come back;
we never again will cross your track
Goodbye, old Bears, good day, and good luck."

*"The Teddy Bears on Broncho backs*
*piled front and back with loaded sacks."*

The sun rose up in a
cloudless sky;
the Bears were ready,
they said goodbye
to friends and trees
and stones and hills,
and with money enough
to pay their bills,
and bags on backs
and sticks in hand,
they started their
tramp across the land.

The Bears were off;
the dust it flew;
the road was wide and
the jockeys knew
that time was short
and the hours were few;
that the night express
was always due
at 5:00 and never late;
if they missed the train
they'd have to wait.

As the train pulled out
the bears sat down
on cushion seats of
velvet brown.
They nodded to men
and ladies too,
and smiled and said,
"How do you do?"

*"Said Teddy-B, 'Pay up the fares,*
*We'll pass tomorrow as millionaires' "*

*"The walking's good and you can go
from here to Chicago by heel and toe."*

"I won't sleep upstairs,"
said Teddy-G., "I want
a window, so I can see."
Teddy-G had fun that
night: he hid the shoes
and put out the light,
and made the porter
keep out of sight,
and saw the cook
and got a bite,
of ham and cheese
and a cup of tea.

The Bears didn't wake
for a day or more;
they missed some meals
about three or four.
When Teddy-G, asked
the porter, when is
dinnertime?
"I am sorry gents,"
said Porter Bill,
but lunch is over and
you fellows will
have to wait right here
six hours at least
before you can have
another feast."

The walking is good
and you can go
from here to Chicago
by heel and toe.
And he put the Teddy
Bears off the train,
on a Kansas farm in a
shower of rain.

As they tramped along to the farmer's yard, the black bear scolded good and hard about the mischief on the Pullman train, and being put off in a shower of rain.

Teddy-G declared that he'd be good if the farmer's wife would give him food; The rules on farms he understood, and he'd do the very best he could.

And they found the farmer splitting wood; and they stepped up bold and said,"Good Day; do you want some hands to plant your hay? We are here to learn the farmers trade; to thresh some wheat or to use a spade. We learn new things at a lively rate and by 6:00 will graduate."

The farmer nearly lost his breath; the two bears scared him half to death.

"The farm is yours," the old man said, "You have the job; now go ahead."

*"We're here to learn the farmer's trade;*
*To thresh some wheat or to use a spade"*

"You milk cows and load the hay,
and hoe potatoes for half a day,
and feed the sheep and plant the corn,
and come to supper when we blow the horn."
The farmer gave them clothes to wear,
and quit his work right then and there.
And asked his neighbors from all-around
to come and see what he had found:
Two bears let loose from a circus show,
or out of a zoo, he did not know.

When at six o'clock the horn it blew,
The Bears said, "Stop! The work is through."
And all hands quit and went their way.
The Bears went round to the house to stay,
to wash their hands and brush their hair,
and get some newer clothes to wear.

A pumpkin pie and jellies sweet,
and other things that farmers eat.
They slept that night in the stable,
and dreamt that they were farmers now,
and had the trade and knew the trick
how farmer boys get ahead so quick.

*"He brought that bull to his knees so quick
he couldn't hook and he couldn't kick."*

The district school was a mile away; the Teddy Bears were free and thought they would go to school for at least a day. The farmer stood at the garden gate, and said, "Goodbye; if you lads are late, the teacher will keep you in at night and give you a thousand words to write."

'Twas the month of June; the day was fine; the children gathered prompt at nine. Teddy-B sat down on the teacher's chair, took off his hat and brushed his hair, and banged the desk and said that he would run the school that day and see that letters danced and figures flew, and that children were good and their lessons knew.

Teddy-G stood just inside the door to check the kids and keep the score;

*"Teddy-B banged the desk and said that he would run the school that day and see."*

*"They walked on ropes drawn good and tight and jumped through hoops and landed right."*

while the teacher sat
on the corner stool
and let the two bears
run the school.
They were glad the day
was finally over.
They asked the children
not to cry, as they put
on their hats
and said good-bye.
They went up the street
to look around; the air
was filled with music
sound; and crowds were
moving here and there,
and flags were floating
in the air.
They walked along to
the public square,
and stepped right into
a county fair.
They rode a donkey
and bought some toys,
and gave them away
to girls and boys.
The children found
them cakes to eat and
asked them home,
their friends to meet.
And three o'clock that
afternoon, a man would
go up in a balloon.
The man was sick; he
couldn't go; and Teddy-B
said, "If that is so, give us
a chance; we'd like to try
a little journey to the sky."

The rope was fastened strong and tight,
the balloon shot up to its greatest height.
The rope was cut and up they flew,
beyond the clouds and away from view.

The balloon sailed up above the crowds
and the county fair and beyond the clouds.
The sky around was clear and blue,
the earth below was lost to view.
The bears sat down to read the books,
and to study maps and examine hooks,
and to learn the way to go up or down,
and how high they were above the town.

We are on short allowance said Teddy-B,
like ship wrecked sailors lost out at sea.
You can have five cakes and two chicken legs
and an apple pie and six hard-boiled eggs
and a loaf of bread and donuts three
and a pound of nuts and a cup of tea."

*"The wind was high and balloon it flew
like a lifeboat sail without a crew."*

"They slid down the ropes and hit the ground
and landed in Chicago safe and sound."

"That's all right," said Teddy-G, "I'll make it do till night is through, but at breakfast time let this shipwrecked crew land on a planet or a twinkling star, or any place where there's a dining-car."

They sailed along at a rapid rate; there were no delays; no place to wait. At break of day there came in view, a pair of cities, and a river too.

They sailed along for hours more; hungry as bears and wet and sore. The storm had cleared; it was growing dark. When passing over Lincoln Park, their anchor caught in a maple tree. "Let us get out," said Teddy-G, "Chicago is good enough for me; I have seen too much of moon and star; I'd rather ride in a Pullman car,

or go on foot or stay right here and eat
and sleep for about a year."

They slid down ropes and hit the ground and landed in
Chicago safe and sound.

They walked around for an hour or two; until they found a
place on a busy street;
a big hotel where there were things to eat.
The food was carried up to their room in style,
above the street about a mile.
Reporters called to get the news about their trip
and to print their views
on Chicago's length and breadth and height,
and what they thought of the town at night.

Two tailors came with cloth and tape to fit them out in
handsome shape. With suits on order and ready made
and vests and ties of every shade.
A barber came to dress their hair; and a manicure, a lady fair,
to brush a paw or trim a nail; and a messenger with the
evening mail. They rested up for several days,

*"Food was carried up to their room in style."*

*Two tailors came with cloth and tape
to fit them out in handsome shape.*

to answer mail and to
learn the ways
of Chicago children
and how to run
an afternoon to give
them fun.

They hired the biggest
hall in town;
Teddy-G said he
would act the clown
if Teddy-B would
run the show,
and explain the tricks
and make things go.

They borrowed
helpers from the zoo,
an elephant & kangaroo,
and six prairie dogs
and monkeys too.
They invited every boy
between 6 years old
and 17; and girls as
many and of equal size,
and for everyone a
handsome prize.
The performing troupe
was hard to beat,
and the crowd which
came filled every seat.

When the show was over
the crowd went wild;
the prizes were given

to every child.
They clapped their hands and danced with joy,
and cheered the Teddy Bears, each girl and boy.

They called aloud for Teddy-G,
when he stepped out and thus said he:

"Chicago's great; I like the place;
it's boys and girls and each happy face."

The Teddy Bears returned to their hotel:
their show was great; they did it well.
The papers praised their work and said
that the Bears were far ahead
in fun and jolly ways
of anything they had seen for days.

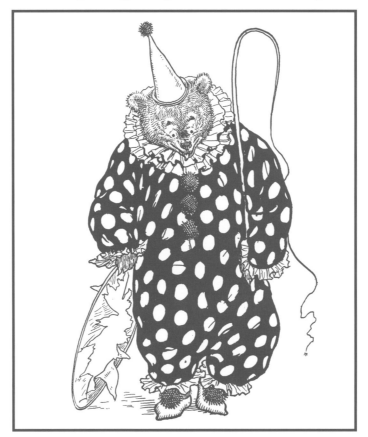

*"But the biggest fun that day
was made by Teddy-G with his clownish play."*

*"It was well worth the trip to see this paper package marked Teddy-G."*

Teddy-B and Teddy-G wanted to go shopping. They walked to one of Chicago's finest department stores and there they got lost, each on a different floor.

Teddy-B walked round the things to see; he hunted and searched for Teddy-G, but he couldn't find him high or low; for an hour at least he was on the go.

He asked some questions here and there, if folks had seen his brother bear.

A floor walker stopped him and said, "Describe his clothes, his height, his walk; his age, his eyes, his face, his talk."

These things he wrote down on a pad and made some signs and called a lad and said, "Take this and go around with this young man to Lost and Found."

The two went off as they were told
and found Teddy-G all neatly rolled
in paper brown and tied with string;
with marks and tags; the funniest thing.
It was worth a trip to see
this paper package marked "Teddy-G ."

The Bears returned to their suite of rooms on the eleventh floor,
where the hotel was filled with flags and flowers;
children were gathering there for hours.
A thousand girls and a thousand boys, laughing and chatting
with merry noise, in parlors, halls, and on the stairs,
to say good-bye to the Teddy Bears.

At seven o'clock they were off again,
to ride once more on a Pullman train.
They raised their hats and said good-bye
to boulevards and buildings high,
to Chicago homes and parks and halls
as their train pulled out for Niagara Falls.

*"The rose is red, the violet blue;*
*these flowers are sweet and so are you."*

"They dressed themselves in rubber suits,
with rubber hoods and rubber boots."

The Bears had heard
of this great resort,
of its fame at home
and at foreign court;
of its bridal parties
and lover's walk,
of its Suspension Bridge
and Prospect Park,
and its Whirlpool Rapids,
Gorge and Cave,
and the battles fought
by soldiers brave.

Their train pulled in at
half-past nine;
the air was warm; the
day was fine.
They started off at
once to view
the rolling rapids and
the big horseshoe.
They sat for a while
on the very brink
while the roaring waters
made them think
of past days and the fun
that they had
and of things they
did a little bad.

They saw the Falls
from every nook,
where tourists stop to
have a look.
They went behind
their guide,
and saw the Falls
from the other side.

"I'm nearly starved; I want to eat;
I want to rest my eyes and feet," said Teddy-G.

"If you'll come with me," said the guide, named Ned,
"I'll find a place where you'll get fed
on doughnuts round and heaps of cake,
and pumpkin pies, my mother's make."
So they ate their lunch all seated round,
on stones and logs on the ground.

After lunch, said Teddy-B, "We must be off;"
"We've a hundred thousand things to see;
we'll send you postcards when we're gone,
to let you know how we're getting on."

As the Buffalo train moved out of sight
the Teddy Bears called back with all their might,
"We leave for Boston town tonight."

*"They started off at once to view
the rolling rapids and the big horseshoe."*

*"They took the books and down they sat
to read Emerson and the Autocrat."*

The Bears will get to Boston soon,
said newspapers that
came out at noon.
They're on their way;
they'll be here at two;
from South Union Depot
they'll drive-through
the city streets
to Beacon Hill,
where their new
friends will
entertain them for
days and nights,
while they are seeing
the Boston sights.

Great crowds had
gathered along the route,
there were girls in
dresses sweet and cute,
and boys with flags
and their teachers too,
for the schools were out
and lessons through.

A jolly crowd, the
Teddy Bears to greet,
to cheer them all
along the street.
The Bears arrived, the
crowds cheered hurray,
the children laughed
the brass band played.
They rambled over to
Copley Square, to
look at the library
building there.

They asked a man
in charge if he
would answer questions,
two or three.
The man said he
would get volumes,
which they could take
away and read.
They took the books
and down they sat
to study Emerson and
the Autocrat.

Said Teddy-G,
"My book's all right,
but it doesn't help my
appetite."
They closed the books
and took them back
and placed them on a
library stack,
and told the man they'd
come again and study
Holmes & Emerson.

The Bears had spent
some strenuous days
in catching up with
modern ways.
But of all the hours
they ever spent
on railroad train or in
mountain tent,
or in balloons on a
stormy lake,
or having picnics of
cream and cake,

*"We've broken something," said Teddy-G.*
*"It's underneath; get down and see."*

*"These gowns and caps and scrolls you see,*
*we give you now as your degree."*

or teaching school or having dinners in a dining car, this ride to Concord was best by far. They hired an auto of latest style, so they could travel many a mile. And through muddy land, a pretty mess while the auto groaned and breathed distress. "We've broken something said Teddy-G. It's underneath; get down and see."

A lad came by on his way from school, who knew autos like a book; he told the bears just where to look. So they were ready to go, the horn they blew, they said thank you, that would due.

Said Teddy-B, on the Concord green, "I'd like to stand up there alone, like that Minute Man on that block of stone."

As guests of honor, the Teddy Bears were invited to Harvard, to speak of their journey east and to enjoy a nice feast.

Two Harvard boys took the Teddy Bears that night
to their college rooms to coach them right,
and to get them ready for their degree:
an L or two and a great big D.

The bears then signed what they had read,
and listened to what the seniors said:
"These gowns and caps and scrolls you see,
we give you now as your degree."

'Twas late next day when the bears awoke
and got through breakfast before they spoke.
They asked the boys to mark the streets down
so they could find their way around town.
They took the list and said that they
would walk from Harvard to the Bay.
They wanted to see Quincy Market on Merchants' Row,
to see if Boston's prices are high or low.

*"I'd like to stand up there alone,*
*like that Minute Man on that block of stone."*

"Teddy-B put a match to a pile of wood
and made a fire and cooked the food."

Then they tramped
down to the wharf to see
the place where patriots
pitched out the tea,
in the year 1723.

"I like this harbor,"
said Teddy-B,
"It's the first time we
have seen the sea;
let us hire a boat and
go down the bay,
and smell salt air to
close the day."

It had a sail and the
wind went west;
they steered their craft
their very best.
They sailed about for
several hours
around forts and
lighthouse towers.
When a storm came up
as black as night,
they tried to turn about,
but the wind was high
and drove them out.

At noon the next day
there came into sight
a tower of ice
all glistening white.

"An iceberg that,"
said Teddy-B,
"Let us hoist our sail
and go and see."

They met a polar bear
who told Teddy-G about the northern pole
and it's size and height,
and the flag that floated there at night,
as well as day:
it was the stars and stripes of the U.S.A.

While Teddy-G told the polar bear
of the United States and the cities there;
of Chicago's streets and buildings tall,
and Niagara River and its waterfall;
of Boston Common and its famous trees,
and Harvard College where they grant degrees.

And down they sat, the hungriest bunch
that ever ate an iceberg lunch.
They spent that night with the polar bear;
they enjoyed the ice and the ocean air.

*"Teddy-B took a turn at the wheel awhile,
and steered the ship for half a mile."*

*"They spent some days in seeing the town: doing Fifth Avenue up and down."*

At breakfast time the following day, a ship was seen a mile away. The polar bear climbed up on high and waved at the ship as it went by. The captain saw the signal fly, and reversed the engines and stopped the ship, asked five sailors to make the trip, and bring on board this ice-bound crew who seemed starved to death and frozen through.

Said Teddy-B, "Take us on board and we'll pay the fare from here to New York or anywhere."

The Teddy Bears walked the ship from bow to stern, and shook hands with children at every turn.

At long last, the Bears arrived in New York, and seeing its buildings high, and how the Bears made money fly, and dressed in style, to see the town, to do Fifth Avenue up-and-down.

The Teddy Bears loved crossing Central Park
for a morning run; or riding subway trains for fun;
and walking Brooklyn Bridge to view
the ships beneath go sailing through.

On the billboards, the bears did see,
a sign that read "Circus Menagerie."
At Madison Garden, with ring and clown,
the biggest thing this week in town.
The Bears were up with the sun next day
to make their plans and prepare the way
for an afternoon of circus play.
They went around at half past eight
to buy the seats at the Garden gate.

"We'll buy the seats if you'll agree
to let us perform," said Teddy-B,

*"Teddy-B and Teddy-G danced a jig for the crowd to see."*

"But the play that caused the biggest laugh
was Teddy-G on a big giraffe."

"We want to try
a thing or two
to show the boys
what bears can do."

"We'll sell you seats,"
the man replied,
"And let you do some
things besides:
You can ride a horse
around the ring,
or act as clowns
or dance or sing,
or lift big weights
or ride a wheel
down a steep incline
on a rope of steel."

But the play that caused
the biggest laugh was
Teddy-G on a big giraffe.

The dancing finished
with laugh and cheer,
and then all the
children on the pier
shook hands with
Teddies-B and G
and asked them both
to come to see
a children's dance,
a pretty sight,
of which they
would give the
following night.

While in the City one fine day, the Bears took a tour bus ride, and they listened to their guide.
The car was open; they enjoyed the air; and they helped the conductor collect the fare.

They went off the bus to buy some roasted ribs and fried potatoes and muffins hot and three cups of coffee in a pot.

As they ate their lunch they heard a ring, both quick and loud: ding! ding! ding! ding!

"A fire! fire!" cried the people on their feet, and the Teddy Bears ran as fast as they could down the street.

They found the fire in a dry goods store and making its way towards three or four of the largest shops on the busiest street: a clothing shop and a store with meat.

*"They climbed up ladders in clouds of smoke, and lifted hose and windows broke"*

*"The crowd of children filled the square;*
*five hundred boys and girls were there."*

There was a great big grocery store on the right and not a fireman yet in sight.

The firemen's hall was across the street and in half a minute came Captain Pete. He told some folks that the job was theirs and had given orders to the Teddy Bears, about the wagons, reel and hose and ladders and firemen's clothes. "Hang onto that nozzle, you Teddy-G, and point it straight at the fire you see. Now let 'er go!" and with swishing stroke the water struck the fire and smoke. And he turned the hose all round about till every fire he could see was out.

There was a report made of the fire that day and the things he heard the towns-folk say about bravery shown and the speed they made of Captain Pete and his fine brigade.

But the jolliest sport of the day began
when they met an organ-grinder man
with a monkey trained to act the clown
and pick up pennies the children threw down.

The crowd of children filled the square;
five hundred boys and girls were there;
and scores of people stopped work to see
the tricks of Teddies-B and G.

The next morning, the Bears were free
to take a River boat to see
the Palisades and Tarrytown
and to view the Hudson up and down.

A request had come from a young cadet
of West Point school, whom the Bears had met.

*"Teddy-G took the crank and just for fun
made marches dance and two-steps run."*

*"Dressed and ready for hours of fun,
with calvary horse or battery gun."*

To dine at the
West Point Army Mess,
and to see the young
people in their
army dress,
or to hear good
stories of army fights
after taps are sounded
to put out the lights.
So they sent a wire to
the cadet to say
that they would call
the very next day.

The boys got out the
flute and drum
and made things all
around them hum,
as they marched ahead
of the Teddy Bears
in army step down the
flight of stairs.

The Bears took the
ferry at half-past four
across the river to the
other shore,
where a train was waiting
to take them down
the eastern bank and
back to town.

The Teddy Bears said
with much regret
that Philadelphia,
they had not seen yet.

The Bears went out to a country place
to see a machine take its trial race;
invented by a New Jersey man
and made to fly on a novel plan.
When the hour arrived to cut the cord,
there wasn't a person who would go on board.

The Teddy Bears said they would make the trip
if only they knew how to steer the ship.

They went over town and farm and creek
in one straight line like a lightning streak,
and it wasn't forty minutes when
they came in sight of William Penn
looking so wise and straight and tall
on the top of Philadelphia's city hall.

*"In Philadelphia, they landed all right on the old man's hat,
where both sat down to have a chat."*

*"We've sailed before," said Teddy-B, "We've hit Chicago down a tree from an old balloon that brought us there, from a little town at a county fair."*

Teddy-B called out
from where he sat,
"There's a man ahead;
I see his hat;
his hand is out;
he means to try
to catch the rope
as we go by."

And as the rope coiled
he pulled with might
and William Penn
he lassoed tight.
A crowd of children
down below
looked up and saw
the Bears let go,
and come from the
clouds like soldiers bold
with not a thing but the
rope to hold.

They landed all right
on the old man's hat,
where both sat down
to have a chat.
And they looked about
and viewed the town
and asked each other
how they'd get down.

The Mayor came out
with a megaphone, and
called up to the tower of
stone, and promised
Father Penn a dime,
if he'd give the Bears
a high old time.

From there they went, the papers say,
to a Broad Street bank to draw their pay,
or to cash a check which Teddy-G
had got in New York as a circus fee.

The Teddy Bears went to the theatre,
where the chairs were filled with fun,
for a boy or girl was in every one.
But the Bears were large and the chairs were small
and they found they couldn't sit at all.
So they stood in the aisle to view the crowd,
and thus spoke Teddy-B out loud:

"Young ladies and gentlemen, children dear,
and chairman too; if there is one here,
Teddy-G and I have come to stay,
to hear and laugh and to see the play.

*"Then he caught one end and with a whirling clip
he showed them how to crack a whip."*

"Across the sand in running dash,
they struck the breakers with a splash."

But since we cannot
very well sit down,
we'll go on the stage
and help the clown."

They made those clowns
march and sing,
and climb up ropes
and through a ring.
And when they finished
there were loud applause
as the Bears ran off
on all four paws.

Said Teddy-B,
"The weather is warm
and sticky too
for fellows dressed
like me and you;
I move we take a little run
down to the shore
for some ocean fun."

So they went off
that very day
to try Atlantic City spray.

They took a ferry to
Camden town
and got a train which
shot them down
across New Jersey
to the sea
so quick they scarcely
had time to see.

They dressed themselves like thousands more
who were walking up and down the shore;
and across the sand in running dash
they struck the breakers with a splash.

They played on the sand with boys and girls,
and ran and danced and had lots of fun,
and dried themselves in the mid-day sun.

Then all the children went on the pier
shook hands with Teddies-B and G,
and asked them both to come and see
a children's dance, a pretty sight,
which they would give the following night.

But the Bears replied
that they must go back to Philadelphia and crackers buy
to celebrate the Fourth of July.

*"Teddy-B and Teddy-G celebrate the Fourth of July.*
*From noon to night they let things go, in the sky above and on earth below."*

*"At the Liberty Bell they took a try,
and hoisted it up both good and high."*

Teddy-G went out the night before
to Market St. to a store,
and bought a load of
sparklers red, and
flags,and kites and toys
to give to each of the
girls and boys.

At the Liberty Bell
they took a try
and hoisted it up
good and high,
and rang it out both
loud and clear,
and at every ring
there went up a cheer.

July the Fourth
is the day that we
who own and love this
country, do celebrate
in smoke and noise,
that we may teach
our girls and boys
that this one day
of every year
is given them free
to shout and cheer.

Said Teddy-G, "I'll
freedom teach
and try to practice
what I preach;
tomorrow I'll let out
the Zoo, the elephants
and monkeys too,
they're just as good
as me and you."

The Teddy Bears went over to the elephant house at the Zoo
and stirred up the biggest elephant, and marched him over to their cake,
before he had time to get half awake.

"You mind these things," said Teddy-G, "Our breakfast hour is half-past three.
If you are good you can have a snack to keep you chewing until we come back."
And they gave old Bolivar (that was his name) some things to eat till back they came.

"We have," said he, "some pie and cake which Teddy-G will undertake
to serve out free in an hour or two to every animal at the Zoo."

The cage was opened and the crowd went out,
monkeys little and big, with laugh and shout,
upsetting each other across the green, the funniest bunch that was ever seen.

From there they went to the animals' cage where they found the tigers in a rage,
and the lions roaring to beat the band in language the Bears didn't understand.

*"Teddy-B made them promise they'd be good, if he'd open the cage and let them out,
and give them an hour to run about."*

"You mind these things," said Teddy-G,
"Our breakfast hour is half-past three."

The Bears took warning
and started back
to find ten zoo keepers
on their track,
and animals both big
and small running
wild on every mall,
and Bolivar with his
trumpet loud
calling for help to
stop the crowd.

But the zoo keeper
made the Bears
change their laugh
when he locked them
up with a big giraffe
and told them to pay
a fine when the police
court met next
day at nine.

When the Bears had
paid their fine
and got outside,
"Let us take a train
for a little ride;
I'm tired of town and
want to see
a farm or stream,"
said Teddy-B.

The fish that day
caught by the Bears
would take first prizes
at all the fairs;

and the way they caught them left and right, and the way they coaxed the fish to bite, and the way they tossed the fish in the air, they landed in trees and everywhere.

The Bears were glad when their work was done to start for the town of Washington, to see the President and shake his hand and then go home as they had planned. When dressed complete and off they went to the house where lives the President. When they reached the grounds and the entrance gate no one was near to make them wait. The news had spread round everywhere of this visit planned by the Teddy Bears. But one little lad who was playing around when he saw the Bears, he stood his ground and stepped up bravely to Teddy-G and said, "Who is it you want to see?" Said Teddy-G in his kindliest way,

*"They met a lad on his way from school, whom they stopped to question about a rule."*

*"With outstretched hand and smiling face, he gave them welcome to the place."*

"We have traveled East and have come today to see the President who doesn't scare and who isn't afraid of man or bear."

The Bears by the lad were keenly eyed, and he said as he beckoned them inside, "My dad's in here; but wipe your feet; I think you're the kind he likes to meet." They stepped inside, and the man they saw looked them over from head to paw and with outstretched hand and smiling face he gave them welcome to the place.

The Bears were asked to come the next day at an early hour to have a play on the White House grounds, in the children's tent and to breakfast with the President.

Said Teddy-B, "Our journey's through; there's nothing left to see or do. We were treated well everywhere we went; and we've met the President. And now for home, that's what I say; but I mean to journey back this way."

The reporters called that afternoon
when they heard the Teddy Bears were going so soon
and begged a column at least of news about their trip and plans and views.
Teddy-B wrote out in the boldest hand these lines that all can understand:

"And to all the people whom we have met please say we leave, with much
regret, for our mountain cave and brook and tree."
Signed,
Teddy-B and Teddy-G

As they crossed the country from East to West they stayed in their sleeping car to rest;
and but once or twice looked out to see the towns passed through and country.
For the news had scattered far and wide when the Bears would reach the mountainside,
And the crowd had come from far and near to welcome back two friends so dear.

They had gifts for each bought in the East
and they passed them round at the evening feast,
and then told stories for nights and days about their trip and the city ways,
and the fun they had and the tricks they played and the things they saw and where they
stayed, and last and best, the time they spent in Washington with the President.

As the Bears turned into their own home nest
and curled up snug for the winter's rest,
said Teddy-G as he fell asleep, "If I should pray for things to keep
of what I've seen either East or West, its boys and girls I like the best."